BABY ELEPHANT GOES TO CHINA

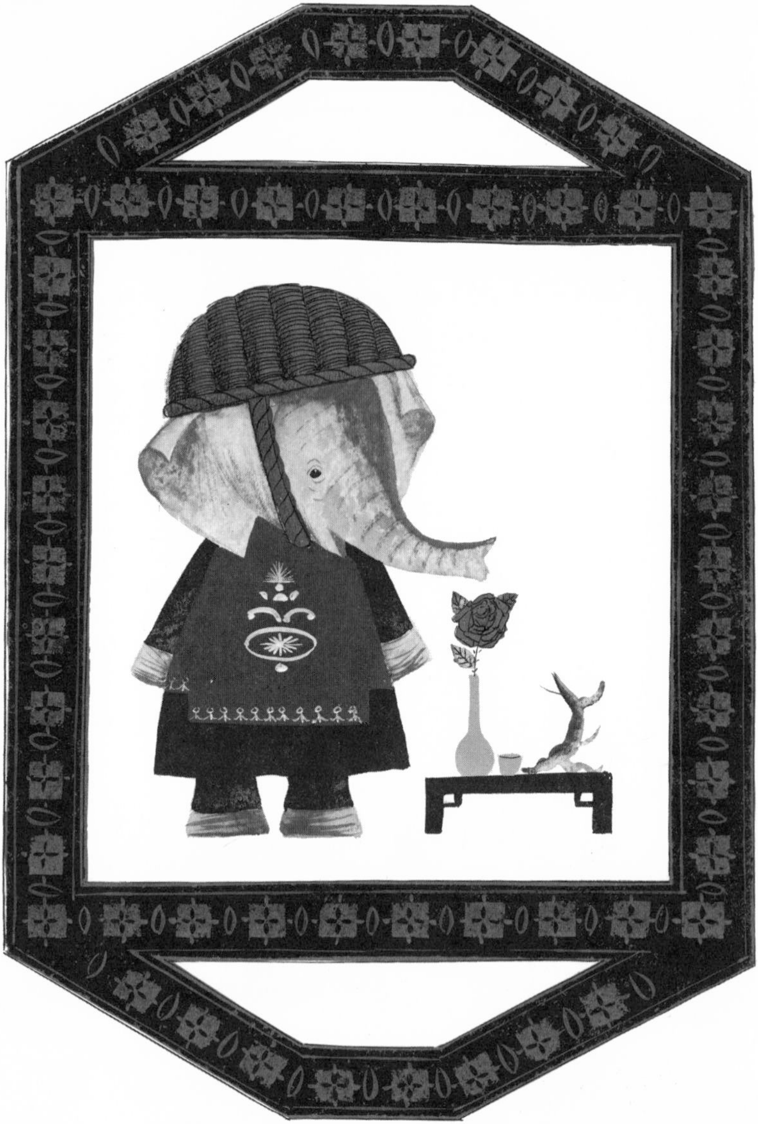

BABY ELEPHANT GOES TO CHINA

BY SESYLE JOSLIN

PICTURES BY LEONARD WEISGARD

HARCOURT, BRACE & WORLD, INC., NEW YORK

Also by Sesyle Joslin and Leonard Weisgard

BRAVE BABY ELEPHANT

BABY ELEPHANT'S TRUNK

SEÑOR BABY ELEPHANT, THE PIRATE

BABY ELEPHANT AND THE SECRET WISHES

Library of Congress Catalog Card Number: 63-15401
Printed in the United States of America
First edition

For

Banana, Pete, and Tom-Tom

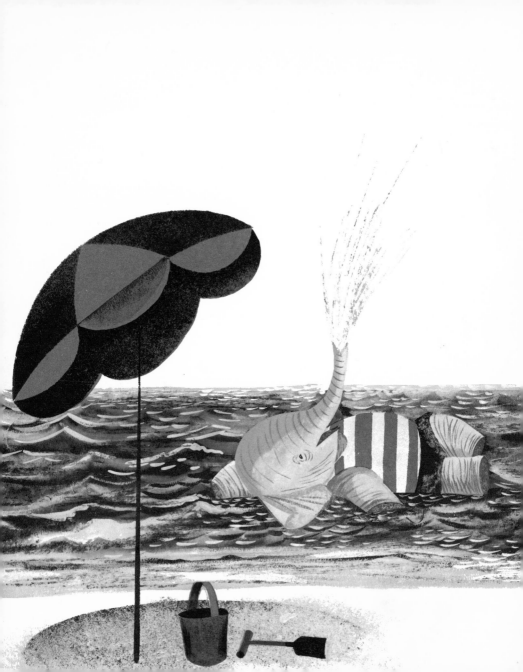

Baby Elephant swam seven strokes one way and seven strokes the other way. He sang to himself as he swam. It was rather a silly song with a good deal of whooshing and trumpeting mixed into it.

"Oh, my trunk's bathing on top of the sea,
And my bathing trunks're on the bottom of me,
*   Whoosh-diddle-dee-trumpet-dum.*
Oh, a rollicking pirate I shall be,
For nobody's got more trunks than me,
*   Whoosh-diddle-dee-trumpet-dum."*

Baby Elephant came out of the ocean, jumping fearlessly over first one wave and then another.

"Whew!" said Baby Elephant. "What a splendid swim that was!" and he trotted briskly up the beach until he came upon a familiar blanket. Here he discovered a large gray body wearing a pair of enormous sunglasses and a great straw hat.

"Is that you, Mother Elephant?" said Baby Elephant.

"It is," said Mother Elephant.

"You are wearing a pair of enormous sunglasses and a great straw hat," said Baby Elephant.

"Yes, I know," said Mother Elephant. "I am sun-bathing *incognito* so that the crowds will not recognize me and shout: 'Look, look! There is the *mother* of the Extraordinary and Remarkable Baby Elephant!'"

Baby Elephant pondered for a moment.

"Mother Elephant," he said, "are you teasing me?"

"Yes," said Mother Elephant, "I am."

"Aha!" said Baby Elephant. "That is just what I thought! And now," he said, sitting down next to his mother, "there is something I have come to tell you."

"What is it?"

"It is I am hungry."

"My dear Baby Elephant," said Mother Elephant, "that is scarcely news. You are always hungry. Sometimes I wonder what you think of beside food."

"That is easy," said Baby Elephant. "I think of *me* beside food. Right beside it."

Mother Elephant heaved and shook with laughter until her sunglasses slid off her trunk. "That is not quite what I meant," she said. "I meant that there is more to the world than food."

"There is?" said Baby Elephant. He was rather surprised.

"It is a fact," said Mother Elephant. "For instance, there is the scenery to admire."

"Well, then," said Baby Elephant, "I shall certainly admire it."

Baby Elephant looked out upon the ocean and gazed up at the sky and peered up and down the beach. Then he lay down and began to sigh in a highly agitated fashion. He caused a good bit of noise and rather a sandstorm as well.

"What is it now?" asked Mother Elephant.

"Now it is this," said Baby Elephant. "Admiring the scenery has only made me hungrier."

"No!" said Mother Elephant, flapping her ears in dismay. "How is such a thing possible?"

"Well," said Baby Elephant, "the sand makes me think of sandwiches, and the water makes me think of watermelon. And do you know, Mother Elephant, do you know what that breaker reminds me of?"

"Good heavens!" said Mother Elephant. "*What* does that breaker remind you of?"

"Of breakerfast," said Baby Elephant, and he rolled over and over, trumpeting loudly. He thought he had made rather a good joke.

Mother Elephant snorted and trumpeted and very nearly blew off her great straw hat. She too thought Baby Elephant had made rather a good joke.

"All right," said Mother Elephant, "all right. I will cook you a snack over the campfire. How do you like your hamburgers?"

"Oh," said Baby Elephant, "I like them very much."

"My silly little elephant," said Mother Elephant. "I know how *much* you like them. I want to know how *done* you like them."

"Oh," said Baby Elephant. "Well done. Naturally."

"And what shall I do now?" asked Baby Elephant when he had finished eating.

"Build a sand castle," Mother Elephant suggested.

"What, another?"

"Collect sea shells," Mother Elephant suggested.

"What, more?"

"Go walking," Mother Elephant suggested.

"But I have been walking for years."

"My dear Baby Elephant," said Mother Elephant, "I have only one other suggestion. It is what I used to do at the beach when I was a baby elephant. It is dig a hole to China."

Baby Elephant furled and unfurled his ears. "Great Scott!" he said. "What an extraordinary suggestion! I am going to China right now, this very moment."

"Godspeed," said Mother Elephant.

Baby Elephant returned. "I am wondering what sort of country China is," he said.

"It is a beautiful sort of country," said Mother Elephant, "with many Chinese elephants and Chinese people riding in rickshas and sailing in junks."

"That is just what I thought," said Baby Elephant, and off he went.

Baby Elephant returned almost at once.

"I forgot something," he said. "I forgot where China is."

"When I last heard," said Mother Elephant, "it was on the other side of the world."

"In that case," said Baby Elephant, jumping around in a delighted way, "everything and everybody in China must be upside down."

"I think perhaps you are jumping to conclusions," said Mother Elephant. "However, I do not really know because I was never able to dig as far as China."

"But you were only a *girl* elephant."

"There's a great deal of truth in what you say," said Mother Elephant. "I cannot deny it."

"Well, do not worry," said Baby Elephant. "I will go to China, and I will come back and tell you all about it."

Mother Elephant adjusted her sunglasses and settled back down under the sun. "I will be waiting," she said.

"Here I go," said Baby Elephant. "Good-by."

"I think you mean to say *tsai-chien*," said Mother Elephant.

"I do?" said Baby Elephant. He was very much surprised.

"*Shih-tê,*" said Mother Elephant, nodding her great head. "*Tsai-chien* is the way Chinese elephants say good-by."

"In that case," said Baby Elephant, "*tsai-chien*, Mother Elephant, *tsai-chien*," and bowing several times in a rather Far Eastern manner, he left.

"Excuse me, please, Honorable Madame Elephant," said a most polite voice at Mother Elephant's other side. She turned, and there she saw a small elephant with a large mustache. It was a handsome and oriental sort of mustache made out of seaweed.

"Good heavens!" said Mother Elephant, considerably startled. "What is this?"

"This is *me*, Baby Elephant!" said Baby Elephant. "And I am wondering how to say some very important words in Chinese."

"What are they?"

"They are soup and cheese and ice cream and peanuts and thank you and perhaps dragon because who knows I just might happen to see one."

"Well," said Mother Elephant, "soup is *t'ang* and cheese is *ju-loh* and ice cream is *ping-ch'i-lin* and peanuts is *hua-shêng* and thank you is *hsieh hsieh* and dragon is *lung*."

Baby Elephant blinked his eyes and flapped his ears.

"By George!" he said. "Why, by George! That certainly sounds like Chinese all right!"

"And what is more," said Mother Elephant, "it looks like Chinese as well," and picking up a long piece of driftwood, she began to write on the sand.

tsai-chien
(good-by)

shih-tê
(yes)

t'ang
(soup)

ju-loh
(cheese)

ping-ch'i-lin
(ice cream)

hua-shêng
(peanuts)

hsieh hsieh
(thank you)

lung
(dragon)

再見
是的
湯
乳酪
冰淇淋
花生
謝謝
龍

Baby Elephant clapped and stamped and trumpeted and roared in quite an enthusiastic way. He was very much impressed.

"Oh, Mother Elephant!" he said. "How do you happen to know so much? Is it because you have such an enormous head?"

"That helps," said Mother Elephant.

Baby Elephant now went about collecting all the necessary equipment for digging a hole to China.

"To begin with," he said, "I shall take Bear.

"And I shall take a shovel because naturally.

"And, of course, I shall wear these," said Baby Elephant, putting a pair of water goggles over his eyes and the picnic basket on his head, "because I always travel *incognito*."

Baby Elephant began to dig a hole to China. He dug and he dug.

"Tell me, Bear," said Baby Elephant. "Will everything and everybody in China be upside down?"

"*Shih-tê*," said Bear.

"That is just what I thought," said Baby Elephant. "You are certainly a wise Bear."

"*Hsieh hsieh*," said Bear.

Baby Elephant continued to dig a hole to China. He dug and he dug. He was beginning to grow rather weary when suddenly he discovered a silver dollar.

"Look! Look!" said Baby Elephant, hopping up and down and causing a sand slide as excited baby elephants are likely to do. "Look! I have found a silver dollar!"

Bear was speechless with surprise and admiration.
Baby Elephant climbed out of his hole and tiptoed past Mother Elephant, who was still sun-bathing. He climbed up the stairs from the beach to the crowded boardwalk. Here there were shops and stands and stalls and other diversions, and here many elephants promenaded up and down.

Baby Elephant approached a small girl elephant who was wearing a flowered beach robe.

"Pardon me," he said, "but would you happen to know the best place to eat?"

"Oh, yes," said the small girl elephant. "The best place to eat is a restaurant."

"My dear little elephant," said Baby Elephant, "I know *what* place is best. I want to know *which* place is best."

"Oh. Well, that is an elegant one," she said, pointing to a nearby café.

Baby Elephant tipped his picnic basket most politely.

"Thank you and good-by," he said.

Baby Elephant went to the café and ordered some food.

"How remarkable!" he said, looking with delight at the soup and cheese and ice cream that the waiter brought to him.

"I am glad that you like it, sir," said the waiter, "and will there be anything else?"

"Oh, yes," said Baby Elephant. "There will be peanuts."

Baby Elephant left the café and walked along the boardwalk until he came to an amusement park. He strolled about for a while, and then he purchased a ticket to ride in a mechanical sort of tin boat.

"Avast and ahoy!" said Baby Elephant, and he gave a spirited salute each time his boat passed the ticket seller's booth. He thought this was an excellent invention.

Baby Elephant left the amusement park and continued his promenade to the end of the boardwalk. There he saw a rather muscular young elephant standing next to a huge chair that had wheels.

"Pardon me," said Baby Elephant, "but would you happen to know what this chair is for?"

"Oh, yes," said the young elephant. "It is for hire. If you hire the chair, you may sit in it, and I shall push you down to the other end of the boardwalk."

"Well, then, I shall certainly hire it," said Baby Elephant, and he did.

Baby Elephant got out of the chair at the other end of the boardwalk. Here he encountered a small lizard.

"How extraordinary!" said Baby Elephant, as he observed the lizard sunning itself.

Baby Elephant went down the stairs and onto the beach. He tiptoed past Mother Elephant, who was still sun-bathing, and he jumped back into his hole.

"Baby Elephant!" called Mother Elephant, several moments later. "Where are you, Baby Elephant?"

"Who, me?" said Baby Elephant, climbing out of the hole with his shovel and Bear. "Why, I have just this very moment returned from China."

Mother Elephant widened her eyes and twitched her trunk. She was astounded.

"What? You have gone all the way to China and back? Great heavens!" said Mother Elephant. "You are certainly a clever baby elephant!"

Baby Elephant nodded his head. He was really rather pleased with himself.

"*Shih-tê*," he said, trumpeting happily. "I suppose I am."

Baby Elephant sat down next to his mother.

"And now," he said, "I will tell you about China."

"As you can see," said Mother Elephant, "I am all ears."

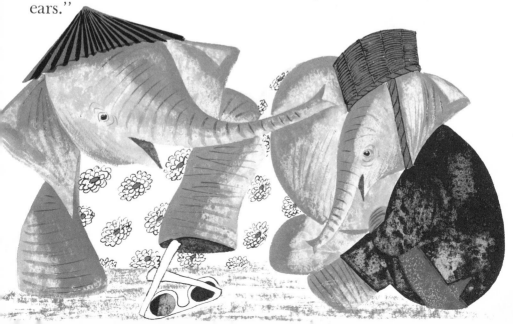

"To begin with," said Baby Elephant, "there was a Chinese elephant girl in a splendid Chinese robe to whom I said *hsieh hsieh* and *tsai-chien*. She was upside down, of course, like everything and everybody in China."

"How remarkable!" said Mother Elephant, snorting in amazement.

"And this is what I did," said Baby Elephant. "I went to an elegant Chinese restaurant, and I ate *t'ang* and *ju-loh* and *ping-ch'i-lin*."

"What, no *hua-shêng?*" said Mother Elephant.

"Oh, yes," said Baby Elephant, "*hua-shêng,* too.

"And then I strolled in a Chinese garden, and then I went for a sail in a Chinese junk! And then I rode through China in a ricksha!"

Mother Elephant's eyes widened, and she gasped for breath.

"What is the matter?" asked Baby Elephant.

Mother Elephant sat very still. "I am spellbound," she whispered.

"But just wait," said Baby Elephant, "wait until you hear this! As I was leaving China, I happened to see an enormous and fierce Chinese *lung!*"

Mother Elephant fell back in a swoon. She made a
tremendous thud and quite a dent in the beach as well.

"And now," said Baby Elephant, "here I am. Right
beside you."

Mother Elephant recovered and sat up. "Yes," she
said, "I see that you are. And I am very glad."

Mother Elephant carefully removed the picnic basket from Baby Elephant's head, and into it she put the water goggles, Bear, and the shovel. Then she folded up the blanket.

"And now," said Mother Elephant, "it is time for us to go home."

"That is just what time I thought it was," said Baby Elephant, "but having dug a hole all the way to China, I am rather tired. Is it possible, Mother Elephant, that you could carry me?"

"Oh, yes, it is possible," said Mother Elephant, and she picked Baby Elephant up in her arms.

Baby Elephant sighed. "It is very nice, of course, to be back again," he said, "but I *do* wish this place were like China with everything and everybody upside down."

"Oh, that, too, is possible," said Mother Elephant, and turning Baby Elephant all around, she carried him by his feet.

"Good heavens!" said Baby Elephant, greatly excited. "How remarkable! How extraordinary! Everything and everybody is upside down! You are certainly a clever mother elephant!"

Mother Elephant nodded her head. She was really rather pleased with herself.

"*Shih-tê*," she said, trumpeting happily. "I suppose I am."

GLOSSARY

tsai-chien (tsy-jee-en)—good-by
shih-tê (shir-teh)—yes
t'ang (tahng)—soup
ju-loh (roo-lah-o)—cheese
ping-ch'i-lin (bing-chee-lin)—ice cream
hua-shêng (hwah-shung)—peanuts
hsieh hsieh (hsee hsee)—thank you
lung (lung)—dragon